This igloo book belongs to:

....

Published in 2013
by Igloo Books Ltd
Cottage Farm
Sywell
NN6 0BJ
www.igloobooks.com

OCE001 0813
2 4 6 8 10 9 7 5 3
ISBN: 978-1-78197-008-9

Written by Sue McMillan
Illustrated by Daniel Howarth

Printed and manufactured in China

Bedtime
Stories

igloobooks

Contents

The Magic Pyjamas

Little Bear was getting ready for bed. "Your old pyjamas are too small," said Mummy, "so I've bought you some new ones."

Little Bear didn't like his new pyjamas. His old pyjamas took him on magical adventures when he went to sleep. Now he wouldn't have any adventures at all.

Little Bear slipped the new pyjamas on. They were surprisingly soft and cosy. He drifted off to sleep and before long, his bed seemed to rock like a boat. As if from far away, he could hear a voice saying, "Captain Moon welcomes you aboard the Starlight."

7

Little Bear opened his eyes. He was on a pirate ship! Captain Moon gave him a real pirate hat. Then, he peered through a telescope and saw a sandy island. "Land ahoy!" he cried. "There's treasure on that island."

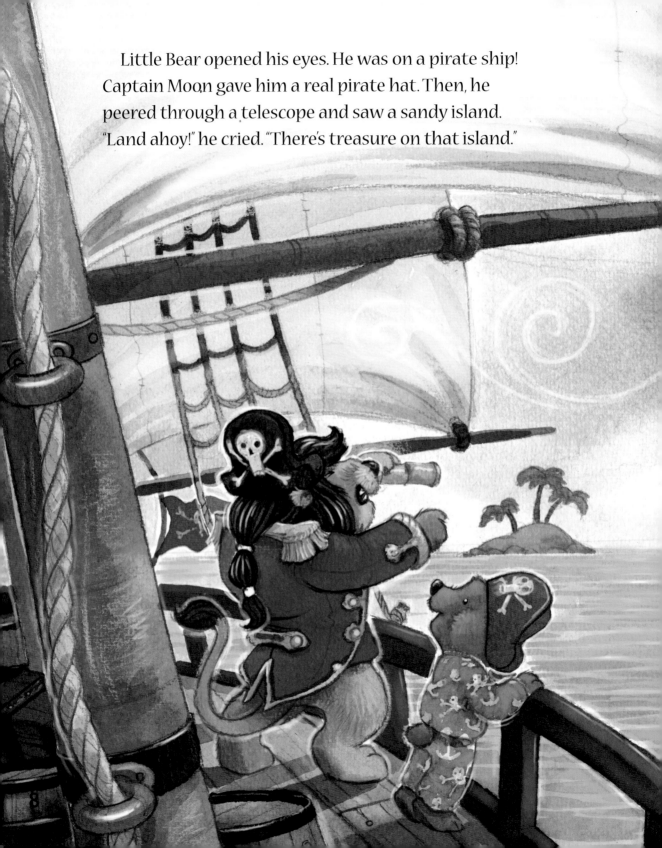

On the island, Captain Moon showed Little Bear an old treasure map. They dug and dug, until they found a chest. Little Bear gasped when he saw the glittering treasure inside, but suddenly, lots of pirates came out of nowhere. "Quick, back to the ship!" shouted Captain Moon.

After escaping from the pirates, Captain Moon and Little Bear looked at all their wonderful treasure. Little Bear picked up a gold coin and gave a big yawn. "You're a brave pirate," said Captain Moon, "but the adventure is over. I think it's time to go home."

When Little Bear woke up the next morning, he ran into
his Mummy's room. "Thank you for my new pyjamas," he said.
"They are even more magic than my old ones!"
"I knew they would be," said Mummy, giving him a lovely hug.
"I can't wait to be a pirate again," thought Little Bear, happily.

Little Stars

Roary Lion and Stripy Tiger played all afternoon in their special tent. They were having so much fun looking at all the interesting things they had found, that they didn't notice the sun beginning to go down.

Suddenly, an owl hooted in the garden. "What's that?" said
Roary, pulling back the tent flap. Outside, it was starting to
get dark. Roary's tummy rumbled loudly. "I'm hungry," he said,
"and I'm scared of the dark. Shall we go inside?"

"There's nothing to be afraid of," said a voice from the garden. It was Mummy and she was carrying a tray of treats and drinks. While Roary and Stripy ate their sandwiches, Mummy explained that the night was full of surprises.

"All sorts of things wake up at night," said Mummy, taking
them outside. A fox crept quietly across the garden, an owl
hooted and bats flitted here and there in the dark.
"Look," said Roary, pointing at the sky. "The moon has woken up."

"The stars have woken up, too," said Stripy, looking up.

Suddenly, a bright star shot across the sky, with a shimmer of dazzling light. "Wow, it's magic!" cried Roary and Stripy together.

"That is the first shooting star I've ever seen," said Stripy, happily.

Then, the two friends began to yawn. "Come on," said Mummy. "It's time for bed." Roary and Stripy agreed. They had enjoyed seeing the night, but being snuggled up in bed with their teddies all safe and warm was even better.

Squirrel's Bedtime

It was bedtime, but Rusty Squirrel was far too excited to sleep. His mummy and daddy had gone out and Curly Cat had come over to babysit. Curly told Rusty to put his pyjamas on, but Rusty just wanted to play and have fun instead.

Rusty went upstairs, but when he came back down, he was
wearing an enormous pair of pyjamas and giggling. "Those look
like your daddy's pyjamas, silly," said Curly Cat, laughing. "Go and
put on your own pyjamas, then come down for your milk."

19

When he had put his own pyjamas on, Rusty crept into the kitchen and grabbed a cookie. Just as he was about to sneak another from the jar, Curly Cat appeared with a glass of milk. "No more cookies, Rusty!" she cried. "It's time for bed."

Rusty still wasn't ready to settle down in bed. He wanted
to play hide-and-seek. He raced upstairs giggling and jumped
inside his toy cupboard, pulling the door closed behind him.
"Curly Cat will never find me in here," he whispered.

Curly Cat knew exactly how to find Rusty, though. Coming into his room, she said in an extra-loud voice, "There won't be time for a bedtime story if I don't find Rusty soon!"

Rusty didn't want to miss his story. He leapt out from his hiding place quickly, yelling, "BOO!"

"Come on, it's time to get into bed," said Curly Cat, laughing.
Rusty climbed into bed and snuggled down. Curly Cat had
only read one page of his bedtime story when he fell fast asleep.
Trying to stay up past his bedtime had been very tiring indeed!

The Bunny Rescue

At the park, Fluffy Bunny wanted to go on the whizzy roundabout, but Hoppy Bunny wanted to play on the climbing frame. They could not agree on what to do. "The roundabout is boring," said Hoppy, and he scampered away.

Fluffy whizzed round on the roundabout with the other bunnies, but when they got off, the roundabout soon slowed down and stopped. "Come and push me, Hoppy!" called Fluffy, but when she looked around, Hoppy had disappeared.

"I'm up here!" yelled a voice. Fluffy looked up and suddenly saw Hoppy waving to her from the very top of the climbing frame. "Come down and play on the roundabout, please?" said Fluffy.

"I want to, but I'm stuck!" cried Hoppy. The climbing frame was very high and Hoppy was too scared to move. He needed Fluffy's help to get down. Carefully, she climbed all the way to the top of the frame and reached out to him.

Together, the friends slowly climbed back down to the ground. "Phew! I thought I was going to be stuck up there forever," said Hoppy, hugging Fluffy tightly. "Come on, let's go and play on the roundabout instead."

As they whizzed around on the roundabout, Hoppy said,
"Thanks for saving me, Fluffy. I couldn't have done it by myself."
"Well, that's what friends are for," said Fluffy, happily. "It's much
more fun playing together anyway!"

Mouse's First Sleepover

Mouse was very excited. It was her first sleepover at her grandparents' house and they had just finished reading a bedtime story. "Goodnight, sleep tight," said Grandpa, kissing her and switching off the light.

Mouse settled down in bed, but the room seemed so
different to her bedroom at home and she didn't like the dark.
"I'm scared," she squeaked quietly and then she began to cry.
Grandpa and Grandma heard and came back to give her a hug.

"Don't worry," said Grandma. "I have something in the attic that might help." Together, they climbed a little ladder into the dusty attic. It was packed full of boxes and funny, old pictures of the family. In the corner there was an old, purple chest.

The chest was full of toys. There was a dolly with woolly hair
and a bouncy jack-in-the-box that sprang up with a boing when
Mouse lifted the lid. "These toys belonged to your mummy," said
Grandma, "and so did this." Grandma held up a teddy bear made
of coloured glass.

"That teddy doesn't look cuddly," said Mouse. "What is it for?"
"Go back to bed and you'll find out," said Grandma, with a wink.
So, Mouse followed Grandma back down the ladder. She ran
into her room and jumped into bed.

Grandpa put the teddy next to the bed and flicked a switch behind it. Suddenly, the room was full of soft, pink light. "Wow," said Mouse, looking at her new night light and smiling happily. "I will never be afraid of the dark again!"

Soon, she was fast asleep. "Goodnight, Mouse," said Grandma.

All the Fun of the Fair

The fair was in town and Cuddly Monkey's daddy had brought her along as a treat. On the carousel, she held on tight to her horse and giggled as it went up and down. Daddy waved from the side as Cuddly went round and round.

When Cuddly spotted the Helter Skelter, she scampered to the top and whizzed all the way down shouting, "Wheee!" Suddenly, she reached the bottom with a BUMP! Daddy was waiting there to give Cuddly a stick of bright, pink candyfloss.

Munching their candyfloss, Cuddly and Daddy went into the Hall of Mirrors. They shrieked with laughter at their funny reflections in the mirrors and made lots of silly faces.
Cuddly was short and wobbly, but Daddy was as tall as a giant.

On the Ghost Train, Cuddly was very brave as they chugged past spooky bats and spiders. Suddenly, a ghost popped out with a loud, "BOO!" Cuddly and Daddy both jumped and Cuddly's sticky candyfloss went all over Daddy's face.

Next, Daddy took Cuddly on the Ferris wheel. It slowly moved round, lifting them high into the air. Cuddly could see all of the lights flashing brightly below them. She leaned against Daddy, happily watching the fair and yawning as the sun set.

It had been a very lovely day but Cuddly felt sleepy.
Daddy talked about what they would do the next time the fair
was in town, but Cuddly didn't hear. She was falling asleep on his
shoulders, dreaming of candyfloss and all the fun of the fair.

Spotty Puppy Explores

Spotty Puppy had a brand new explorer's outfit. "I'm going on an adventure, Mummy," he called and dashed out of the door. "Don't get too dirty and come back before it gets dark!" called Mummy, but Spotty wasn't listening, he was already on his way.

Something was hissing near the hedge. "Maybe it's a snake," said Spotty, creeping closer. "Got you!" he shouted, grabbing the hissing thing, but it just squirted water at him. "Urgh!" cried Spotty. "I'm all wet. It's not a snake at all, it's the garden hose."

43

Spotty was drying himself off when he saw something stripy, wiggling among the flowers. "Maybe it's a tiger," he said, crawling closer. He reached out and grabbed the wiggly thing tightly. "Miaow!" the wiggly thing cried, jumping up in fright.

Spotty had grabbed hold of the cat's tail. He got such a shock, he stumbled backwards and landed, SPLAT, in a very muddy puddle. "Oh, no!" cried Spotty. "Now I'm all wet and dirty."

It was getting dark, so Spotty decided to go back inside.
He pushed his way through the bushes just as Mummy was
opening the door. "Aaargh!" she cried, when she saw him.
"It's a monster!"

Then, Mummy realised it was Spotty. He was all muddy and covered in leaves. "Spotty, you've given me such a fright," she said, laughing. "You look more like a jungle monster than an explorer! Come on, let's get you into a nice, warm bath."

Soon, Spotty was splashing in a lovely bubble bath. He played with his yellow duck and his submarine. "I love being an explorer," he said. "Tomorrow, I'm going to find a real jungle monster!"

"Of course you are," said Mummy, and she gave Spotty a big hug.